Matchmaker Bride

SMALL-TOWN BRIDES

DIANA LESIRE BRANDMEYER

For all of those looking for the right forever love

Contents

CHAPTER 1

EMMIE MUELLER WORE HER favorite floral dress to the July wedding. She hoped the skirt wouldn't wilt in the humidity. Two old bachelors down and two to go, and then she and Granny would be on their way to Kansas to be with their family.

Orville Tinze, the first bachelor she made a match for, had bluebonnet eyes and soft manners, which made him attractive to several older widows. In less than a month, he said his vows.

Getting today's happy couple together had been the most difficult task. A nigh impossible endeavor. But with God's help, she'd found a wife for George Henderson. One Sunday, she noticed the church organist, spinster Louise Wheeler, sending longing looks toward George. The surly old man would never have picked up on those subtle glances. But Emmie did, and she took action.

With a little coaxing, she managed to get George looking quite dapper before she put the two of them together at the church voters' meeting. He took to Louise like rain on a parched garden.

Finding the other two boarders a spouse couldn't be as tiresome. Her cheeks hurt from smiling.

"Do you take. . ."

She brought her attention back to the vows. This had to be the best part of the wedding, when two people in love promised to be together forever. And to think, God used her to bring this about. This must be God approving her plan to find matches for the other gentlemen boarders.

Hylda Mueller, Emmie's grandmother, nudged her in the side and leaned close to her ear. "Someday that will be you."

A rush of heat rose to her face. "Shh, Granny." Sometimes her grandmother spoke too loud, and when Mrs. Thompson snickered behind them, Emmie feared this was one of those times.

Granny patted her leg and nodded.

The couple faced the congregation, and the pastor introduced the newlyweds. Both of them beamed through their wrinkles. Satisfied everyone had their attention on the couple, Emmie slipped out the side of the pew. The finishing touches for the reception being held in the side yard of the church needed to be readied.

⁓ele⁓

Landon Knipp left the building he was considering renting in Lebanon, Illinois, thankful his father had come along with him to inspect it. This one, unlike others they'd explored, appeared to be the right size for his specialty market and in the right location on the corner of Main and Spruce.

Mr. Knipp brushed dust particles from his jacket sleeve. "You don't need to move. Why not stay in St. Louis and work with the family? It's a headache to start a new place where you aren't known."

"Father, whether you believe it or not, as the youngest, I'll never have a chance to be the boss. I've spent my entire life being ordered around by my brothers. I'd like to try being the one in charge." Landon stepped back to inspect the front overhang. "No light peeking through."

"Where do you plan to live?"

"Maybe above the store. That would give me a bit more money to put into this place, maybe on better display cases." Landon shaded his eyes and peered down the busy street crowded with farm wagons and buggies. Another good indication that his store would have customers.

Church bells jangled in an unordered tune, as if a few schoolboys had control of the rope.

"Is it the top of the hour already?" His father checked his pocket watch. "No, not even close. There must be something happening at the church."

"Sounds like it's around the corner. Let's walk in that direction. This building is only one part of my life. I'll need to find a church. Worshipping is important as well."

And finding a wife.

All six of his married brothers had at least one child. When he'd returned from Europe, he'd been surrounded by infants and toddlers. Each one brought a distinct desire in him to have a family of his own. And to stay in one town. No more traveling for him.

If the bells didn't lead them to church, the steeple would have. The redbrick building was simple in appearance except for the stained-glass, circular window above the double entry doors. Though it wasn't as grand as those in Europe or back East. Even St. Louis had more impressive houses of worship.

The side yard contained tables decorated with many different cloths and flowers. "I'd say it's a wedding." Landon stopped at the bottom of the steps.

The door flew open. A blond-haired beauty hurried through it and down the steps.

"Do you suppose that's the bride?" His father snickered.

Emmie's narrow-skirted dress hindered her movement. Now she regretted wearing it, instead of the wide skirt she wore at home. Going slow down the stairs wasted time. She needed to uncover the food.

On the last step, she stumbled.

Her ankle twinged.

She grasped for something to steady herself, but found air.

Someone grabbed her by the waist, and she fell into the arms of a man. One she'd never met. Emmie swallowed. Was her embarrassment from the fall? Before she could sort out her feelings, he righted her and then tipped his hat.

"Landon Knipp."

"Thank you for saving me, Mr. Knipp. I'm afraid my mind was on getting the tables ready for the wedding guests." She smoothed the skirt at her waist.

"Then you aren't the bride?"

She hadn't noticed the older man standing next to Mr. Knipp.

"Father. Excuse him, Miss. . . ?"

"Miss Mueller." She turned to the older gentleman. "No, sir, I'm a helper today."

"My father has an odd sense of humor."

"I see. Well, if you don't mind, I need to get busy." She took a step and winced. "Ow."

He grasped her by the arm. "Here, lean on me, and I'll get you to the tables. You can sit and rest and direct Father and me on what needs to be done."

"I couldn't, shouldn't. . ."

"She's right, son. We aren't guests at this wedding."

"We won't stay. With the two of us, we'll get things shipshape in no time. Miss Mueller?"

If they hurried, there might be a chance. And she did want George and Alice to have a beautiful day. "Please, that would be kind of you, and then you can be on your way." They would have to finish before Granny saw him, or there'd be wedding suggestions before they made it home. Having a new man in town would ignite the fire under Granny, and the pressure to marry would be upon her once again.

CHAPTER 2

LANDON UNCOVERED THE THIRD dish of potato salad and moved it down to a table next to the other two bowls. That was the last one. He stepped back to inspect the display. Finished and grouped like with like. He and his father did a decent job of making the tables appealing. A feast for the stomach and the eyes. Would Miss Mueller think so? He glanced at her. She rubbed her ankle. It would be blue and purple by evening.

A loud cheer rose from the front of the church. The newlyweds and their guests would be coming this way soon. He headed over to Miss Mueller. "We're finished. Is there anything else you'd like us to do?"

"You've done a marvelous job. I wouldn't have considered placing the foods the way you have. We usually let the person bringing something set it where they want it."

"It makes more sense to have all the potato salad in one place, doesn't it?" He scratched his chin.

She wrinkled her forehead and chewed her lip.

"Unless there is a reason?"

"There is. It's a tradition passed down from generations. If one has all the bowls together, someone might get their feelings hurt if their bowl isn't touched. And sometimes people forget to put something on their plate, and they have a second chance of doing so as they move down the row."

"We should move them around then. I'll get Father—"

Her eyes widened, and she looked past him.

"Emmie, who is this?"

He turned to find an older woman standing behind him. "I'm Landon Knipp, ma'am. My father and I helped Miss Mueller set out the food."

"They aren't staying, Granny. They offered to help when I misstepped and twisted my ankle." She stood, wobbled, and caught the edge of the table to steady herself.

"Nonsense. You helped my granddaughter, and you must stay. There's plenty of food." The older woman beamed. "We love having new people attend our church. Where are you from?"

"St. Louis." His father stepped next to him. "My son is looking at a building to open his new business."

"What do you do, Mr. Knipp?"

"If I decide to settle here, my store will carry items you can't find at the mercantile. My father owns Knipp Emporium in St. Louis. And I'm opening our second one."

"What does that mean? Things I can't find at the mercantile?" Emmie narrowed her eyes.

Landon's heart stuttered. He'd insulted her town and her. "Items from all over the world. Fine china, exotic spices from India, that sort of thing. When a customer walks in, we want them to be wide-eyed and speechless while they take in the displays."

"Followed by excitement. Don't forget that, Landon. Lest the ladies think you want them to be as quiet as a church mouse while they shop." His father chuckled.

"You won't be competing against the mercantile, then?"

"Not at all. Our intent is to have different choices. Not everyone gets to travel around the world purchasing items to decorate their homes or give as gifts. Like this." Landon pulled a handkerchief stitched with embroidered birds from his pocket and handed it to her.

She traced the stitching. "It's beautiful. You're right. I haven't seen anything like this before."

"Our store will be filled with items like this."

"Look, Granny, isn't this exotic?"

Mrs. Mueller held it in her hands and rubbed the fabric between her thumb and finger. "The fabric is soft as down."

"You will do well with a store in this town. When will you decide?" Mrs. Mueller cocked her head. "And where do you plan on living?"

❦

Emmie knew what was coming before Granny asked. She wanted a boarder to fill George's room. "Granny! That's none of our business."

"It certainly is. Did you forget we run a boarding-house?"

She squirmed like a little girl under Granny's glare. "No, but remember—"

"This is not the time or place to discuss this." She turned to them. "If you are in need of a place to stay, please come see us. We have plenty of rooms available."

Rooms she'd worked hard at emptying of boarders. She knew Granny didn't want to leave this town, but it wasn't fair of her to expect Emmie to stay here. She wanted to be with her family, and that included Granny. Yes, she did want to marry and have children, but not here. No, she did not. She wanted to be near her momma. But Momma wouldn't approve of her pouting. She gathered her emotions and tucked them away.

"Mr. Landon, it would be an honor if you'd stay with us for a short time." *Please turn down the offer.*

"Thank you, but Father and I will return to St. Louis this afternoon. I have some decisions to make. I've seen several towns that fit my needs."

His words were like warm butter, and the tension in her shoulders dissolved. A problem diverted, though looking at him again, it wouldn't be hard to find him a wife if he did stay. Handsome, with those Jersey-cow eyes framed with long, dark lashes. Yes, there would be a few women in town that would want to sit at his table every night. Good thing he was leaving, because she might be tempted to get his attention and that would mess up her plan.

There were quite a few people at the reception. Landon listened in on conversations as he filled his plate, hoping to get a feel for the people of the town.

"Something's going on, Walter. I think Emmie is up to some shenanigans."

Hearing Emmie's name, he whipped around and took note of the two older men behind him in line.

"Milton, I'm telling you. Orville getting married didn't surprise me. He still has all his hair. But George? Didn't you notice how Miss Emmie got him to slick down his hair and make sure his mustache didn't have food in it every Sunday?"

"You might be right. Do you think she's trying to match us up, too?"

"We best keep an eye on her. I like things the way they are." Milton plopped potato salad onto his plate.

"Landon?" His father spoke into his ear. "You are listening in on conversations again?"

"Yes. You can learn a lot about the culture of a place when you do that."

"You're in Illinois, son, not a foreign land. Not much different from where you grew up. Let's look for a place to sit."

Under a young tree, they found a spot that hadn't been claimed and settled beneath it with their packed plates. From here, Landon observed Miss Emmie Mueller undetected. Her delicate fingers piano-key danced through the air while she chatted with another woman.

"She's a pretty one with that blond hair." His father wiggled his fork in her direction. "Are you thinking this town might offer you more than a place to sell wares from abroad?"

"You know me too well. But it's not just her. I know nothing about her. It's the townspeople that will be the key to having a successful business. Like those celebrating this wedding. I should think them to be an indication of the type of people I'd be selling to."

Miss Mueller filled her own plate even with an injured ankle. He noticed. Yes, he did. He'd been watching for a beau to offer her assistance, but none came. Maybe she didn't have one. Curious that one so beautiful wouldn't have a group of bachelors hanging around trying to capture a smile from her.

"—and you'd need furniture, too." His father's words broke into his thoughts.

"Pardon? My mind drifted somewhere."

"I thought as much. I've been observing your keen interest in the young Miss Mueller. Your fork has been hovering over that piece of ham for quite some time." His father raised his eyebrow. "What interests you the most about her?"

He stabbed the piece of meat and stuck it in his mouth, debating whether or not to answer his father's question.

"You're stalling, son." He laughed loud enough for a group to turn and stare.

Landon tipped his hat at them. "She must be a member of this church, as she is talking to everyone. One of my high priorities. I desire a marriage such as my brothers' and yours. This might be the best town we've seen to open the store." And Emmie Mueller, the possible matchmaker, was the first woman he wanted to get to know.

CHAPTER 3

Emmie held a bowl of green beans as she settled in the rocker between Milton Taylor and Walter Hoffman. She picked one up and snapped it. The ends fell onto her apron. "What did you two think of the wedding?"

The rockers creaked against the wooden porch floor.

Emmie stared at Milton.

He stopped rocking. "Did you say something?"

"I asked what you two thought of George getting married?"

The rocker resumed its motion at a quick pace. "Don't see what that old grump needed a wife for."

Walter leaned forward. "Me either, Milton. Mrs. Mueller takes good care of us, and we don't have to do anything. Now George will have to do everything his wife wants."

"That's not nice. George is happier than both of you. Did you see him smiling at the wedding?"

"Of course, he was. There were tables of pie waiting for him after the ceremony."

Emmie ignored Milton. "Just think, he will have someone to listen to him at dinner."

"We heard everything he said." Milton snorted. "Even when we didn't care to."

"Never said much worth hearing." Walter nodded. "No sir, that man is going to run out of interesting things to say before next Sunday."

The door opened, and Granny leaned out. "Emmie, can you run and get me some baking soda? I'm plumb out, and I need it to make the biscuits for dinner."

"Yes, ma'am, I'll be happy to." She gathered the hem of her apron in her hand as she stood. "Sitting with these two makes me sad. They don't have a romantic bone in their bodies." She shook her apron over the porch railing.

"We're too old for that foolishness. Set in our ways." Walter settled back against the rocker. "But you're not, missy."

Emmie spun on her heel. "I have plenty of time once I get to Kansas." But did she? Her age was creeping up fast. What if she didn't find someone to love there? *Dear God, is it Your plan for me to be a spinster?* Her stomach sank. If it was, could she follow it?

Landon's gut instinct was right four weeks ago, when he'd first visited this town. It would be a good place to open his store. And a lovely blond woman had something to do with it as well. He closed and locked the door to the new store and pocketed the key. His stomach growled. He needed to find a place for breakfast. Last night convinced him he had no desire to sleep above the store. The old bed creaked with every breath he took and disturbed his sleep until his body gave up and he drifted off.

This morning, the sun broke through the dirty upstairs window, waking him. He missed the smell of coffee wafting up to greet him. Not to mention a plate of eggs and a muffin. He hadn't noticed the lack of a kitchen before he bought the place, and the idea of buying a stove and all that went with it didn't appeal to him. Plus, his cooking wasn't fit for hogs. He could purchase a new bed and eat his meals out, but the cost would add up fast. It might be best to find a boardinghouse.

The scent of bacon tugged him down the street to the Maisie's Diner. As he entered, several diners turned in his direction. Some nodded, others went back to their conversations. He slipped his hat from his head and relaxed his shoulders, happy that his first foray into his new world wasn't going to be confrontational.

"Find yourself a place to sit, and I'll be there directly to take your order." The waitress pointed at a few empty tables and went back to filling coffee cups.

Finding the table close to the window appealing, he settled in to watch the comings and goings of people. He hoped he'd picked a community who would enjoy and purchase unusual gifts possessing novelty and individuality. But if he chose wrong, he would be back on a train to

St. Louis to spend the rest of his days being the low man, bossed by his older brothers until he died.

A woman walked past. He noted her plain clothing and decided she wouldn't be a likely customer. A few more people strolled by, heads bent and in a hurry to get to work. What if they couldn't afford what he planned to sell? He would need to place an order for some of the less expensive trinkets. This wasn't St. Louis where he could count on selling to one class of people. He wanted everyone in this town to be able to purchase at least one or two special things from him.

He'd send a telegram this morning after his first shipment was delivered.

"What would you like this morning?" The waitress plunked a coffee cup on the table.

"Scrambled eggs, bacon, and toast to go with the coffee. I'm looking for the boardinghouse that the Mueller's run. Do you happen to know if they have a room open?"

The waitress nodded as she filled his cup. "Yes, I do. A gentleman left last week, and I don't think the room's been let yet. You might want to get yourself over there early today as the Muellers are known for their spread. Guess that means we won't be seeing you here once you taste her granddaughter's muffins."

Miss Emmie Mueller, the girl who haunted his dreams, the one who made him choose this town to settle down in.

"Anything else?"

The waitress pulled him away from the blond-haired beauty in his mind. "Just the address of the boarding-house."

CHAPTER 4

Emmie, at her grandmother's insistence, had the afternoon to go play with her friends. She giggled. Imagine being told at eighteen to do that. The problem was, there weren't any schoolmates to play with. Except for Alice, all of Emmie's school friends had married or moved to other towns.

Her friend lived on the opposite side of town from the boardinghouse. Emmie delighted in the walk, because the late-July weather somehow found a bit of coolness to share. It was nice to be away from the boardinghouse. Since her parents left for Kansas, she and Granny worked harder to keep everything cleaned and polished. Kansas would be a relief for both of them.

And they wouldn't have to take care of Walter and Milton. She stopped walking and turned back to the store she'd passed. She might as well get a spool of thread as they were almost out. Before breakfast, Walter brought down two shirts that needed buttons sewn on. She nor Granny could figure out how he managed to break the threads that held them. Every week he brought down a shirt, buttons in his hand, and delivered it to Granny for repair. Emmie watched him for a week, to no avail to see if he was twisting them off while he rocked on the porch.

While she was in the mercantile, she picked up a pack of needles. Since her parents left, she'd been purchasing small supplies to take to Kansas. With her mind on her ever-growing packing list, she stepped out of the store and bumped into a man hard enough to knock her off balance.

Hands steadied her.

"Miss Mueller. I didn't expect to be catching you again."

It was him. Mr. Knipp. Her body heated. It must be from the July weather and not him. She searched for words.

"My apologies. I suppose that wasn't the correct thing to say."

"No. No, it's fine. I'm surprised to see you, and yes, thankful once again that you saved me from a fall. You decided to open your store here?"

"I did. After meeting so many kind people at the wedding picnic, I couldn't think of a better place to reside. May I walk you somewhere?"

"I'm on my way to a friend's home. It isn't far. She just got married a few weeks ago. I'm running late." Goodness, she sounded like a fool. The man didn't need to know how long Alice had been married.

"Good day then. I hope to see you around. Sunday at church, perhaps?"

"Yes, I'll be there."

"Sunday then. My pleasure to catch you today." Mr. Knipp smiled and headed down the street. She let go of the breath she didn't know she'd held and quickened her steps. Alice would know what to do about these unexplained feelings she had when Mr. Knipp caught her.

"Miss Mueller, how is your mother?"

Emmie paused. She hadn't noticed Mrs. Diekman leaning against the picket fence.

"Have you had a letter from her? I miss seeing her at church."

"I'm sure she misses you, too. We had a letter last week. Father is scouting the land while they stay in town. Mother says it's quite delightful to be the boarder for a change, though she feels guilty about sitting around and not waiting on others."

"I imagine she does. I don't remember her sitting still often. Are you off to visit Alice?"

"Yes, it's been a while since we've spent time together." Because Alice was married and she wasn't?

"Make time for your friendships, dear. You never know when one of you will move."

Emmie bit her lip. She would be leaving soon. Would she ever see her friend again? Or Mr. Knipp?

Landon helped carry heavy wooden crates from the wagon into the storefront. He intended to sort them as the boxes came in, placing each in the area designated for the type of merchandise inside. Except the driver arrived without any help. Landon slipped off his coat and rolled up his sleeves. It wasn't the first time he'd unloaded a wagon, and owning a store meant it wouldn't be the last time either.

"That's all of them." The driver set down the small trunk he carried and rubbed his back. "What do you have in these crates, anyway?"

"Unusual items that can't be found in this town." Landon surveyed the store. The wooden display shelves across both walls would hold a lot. Then there were the cases with glass shelves. Did he order enough to fill the empty places?

"What kind of items?"

"Imported parasols and silks from China, along with other quality pieces."

"Sounds pricy. Don't know how well that sort of thing will sell around here. Mostly farm folks live here, and they aren't likely to buy fancy pieces of material."

"I'll place an order for some less expensive things." He'd do it right away because once word got out that his wares were costly, no one would come in to look. He scratched his head. He could make certain pieces look more expensive by displaying one or two things on a shelf. He'd suggested that to his father once, and his brothers laughed. "Why not display everything?" became the taunt of that summer. That's when he'd decided to be the buyer, leaving home, traveling to Europe for the best things. And to get away from her.

Breathing hard, Emmie banged on Alice's door.

"What's wrong?" Alice pulled her friend inside.

"He picked our town."

"Who? I'm lost."

"Mr. Knipp. The man who kept me from falling down the church stairs at George's wedding. And today, today I ran into him coming out of the mercantile."

"That's nice that you saw him again."

"No, not saw. Crashed into him. I lost my balance, and once again he saved me from disaster."

"Why does this matter to you?" Alice guided her into the parlor and sat on the sofa. "Sit and tell me what the problem is."

"He's handsome, and when he had his hands on my waist—" Oh glory, her face was on fire.

Alice giggled. "You like him. That's wonderful!"

"But I'm moving."

Alice poured tea into a cup and handed it to Emmie. "Yes, you've said that for months now."

Emmie knew where Alice would go next. She took a sip of tea from Alice's delicate wedding china cup. She needed to change the subject fast. "This is beautiful. Are you happy with this pattern?"

Alice traced the rim of her cup. "I think so. It was hard to pick one I wanted to live with for the rest of my life. Still, sometimes, I think about my other choices. I'll admit to that. Mother says eventually, I'll forget about them."

"I think you did well both in china and husband picking." A twinge of jealousy pricked her mind, but she banished it. After all, what good would a set of pretty china thin enough to see through be in Kansas? It would break before they arrived.

"When are you leaving to meet up with your family?"

"Soon, I hope. Once I find matches for Mr. Hoffman and Mr. Taylor, Granny and I can pack the house and leave."

"Are you traveling alone?" Alice scrunched her face. "I wouldn't care for that at all. It's so much nicer to travel with a man."

"I'm capable, as is Granny, of getting on and off of a train. Father will meet us with a wagon. Granny says not to anticipate problems."

Alice shook her head. "Does she ever worry?"

"I've not seen any sign of it, except for getting the meals on the table on time. If she has concerns about other things, she keeps it between her and God."

"I wish I could be more like that. I can't stop worrying about everything." She stared into her cup.

"Is something wrong?"

"No. It's that I want a family." Her face reddened. "I shouldn't talk of these things with you."

"So society would dictate. But I'm your friend. Tell me."

Alice set her cup on the saucer. "We've been married for three months, and I should be expecting by now."

"Have you talked with your mother?" Emmie had no idea how long it took for such things to occur.

"Yes, she said it takes a while for some, and for others it doesn't. I'm not supposed to fret about it but enjoy my time without children because they will come soon enough, and I'll never have a moment's peace."

Emmie gasped. "She said that?" A giggle bubbled up and broke through, followed by more. "I'm sorry."

Alice joined her. They laughed until their eyes teared and tea sloshed over Alice's cup.

"I'm going to miss you so much. You will write to me, won't you?" Emmie set her cup and saucer on the table.

"Of course, but you must answer. I want to know everything about your new life. Do you suppose we'll see each other again?"

"I'll see you this Sunday at church."

"I meant after you leave." Alice's lip trembled. "Why don't you marry and live here? Our children would be friends, and we would never complain about not having a moment's peace."

"I've told you why. It's hard to leave, but I want to be with my family. Besides, I don't even have a beau."

"It's because you're too picky."

"I'm not. God hasn't put the right person in front of me, that's all." For a brief moment, the concern in Mr. Knipp's eyes tugged at her heart. He'd been in her path twice now. She pushed it away. "The boys we went to school with are still boys in my mind. I don't want to find a toad on my table or my chair covered with honey."

"The honey on the chair never happened. You do understand they are now men, and most aren't mean. They regret calling you Monkey Arms. Some even apologized to you, including my husband."

"I know, but I can't forget how they made me feel. No, I think I'm supposed to marry someone I don't have a history with." *Right, God? That's what you've put on my heart, isn't it? That's the reason the rest of my family moved so far away. My husband is waiting in Kansas, right?*

CHAPTER 5

Landon walked the few blocks to the boardinghouse the waitress recommended. A wide wraparound porch skirted the redbrick building. Its chairs and rockers beckoned him to sit and relax. White shutters hugged the windows, secure enough to withstand a tornado. He knocked on the door and stepped back when it opened.

"It's you, Mr. Knipp. The young man who helped my granddaughter set up for the wedding. How delightful to see you again. Please, come in." Mrs. Mueller stepped aside and wiped her hands on her apron.

He slid his hat from his head. "I've come to see if you have a vacant room to let."

"It just so happens we do. My Emmie wants to empty this place out, but not me. I like having boarders. How long will you be staying?"

"Once I get the store open, and it's running well, I intend to buy a house. So, I'm not sure. A month? Maybe two? Depending on the cost."

Mrs. Mueller gave him a price. It was cheaper than buying a bed and the cost of meals. "I'll take it."

"You look tired. Haven't you been sleeping well?"

She reminded him of his grandmother. Caring for others and seeing to their needs was her way of life. "I spent last night above the store on an old creaky bed. I couldn't find a moment of silence to slide into sleep." He rubbed the back of his neck where the muscles from moving boxes were making themselves known.

"That settles it, then. You'll get your things and be back here by dinnertime. Tonight, you'll rest and wake ready to tackle setting up your store. Before you go, let me get you a few of Emmie's cookies to take with you. She's quite a good baker."

While he waited, his curiosity took over. He inspected the part of the home he could see. Nothing exotic or imported in the parlor.

"Here you are, Mr. Knipp. You snack on these. They should perk you up. Be back here by five. That's when we serve dinner. You can meet the other boarders then."

The scent of vanilla and butter from the cookies smelled of home. The only thing that would make them better was if Emmie were here herself.

Emmie let the screen door bang behind her. She unpinned her hat and hung it on a peg, then grabbed the apron next to it. "I'm so sorry for being late, Granny." She took a paring knife from the drawer and picked up an empty bowl.

"Slow down. You'll cut yourself." She carried a bowl of washed potatoes to the table. "I've scrubbed them clean for you."

"Thank you. You shouldn't have had to do that." She sat in a chair and spread the apron over her lap.

"I'll sit and watch you peel those while you tell me all about your visit." Granny poured two glasses of tea and set them on the table.

Emmie took a drink. "That tastes good. It's so hot today, and I walked fast." Her grandmother gave her the familiar look that often put Emmie in her place when she was small. "I didn't run, but I did work up a thirst. Thank you for the tea."

"I'm glad to know on Sunday I won't hear about you running like a boy to get home."

"I'd not embarrass you. Alice is doing well. She likes having her own home." Emmie set to work on the potato skin. A thin brown ribbon spiraled to her lap. "We promised to write when I go to Kansas."

"I don't imagine you'll need to put pen to paper soon. I took on another boarder this afternoon. The poor man wore his tiredness in his face."

"A new boarder?" Emmie could lay on the table and cry. Now she had three wives to find. *Why God? Why are you keeping me from my family?*

"Why would you take in a new boarder? Don't you want to be with everyone in Kansas? Don't you miss them the way I do?" She gathered the peelings into the center of her apron and dumped them in the bucket by the door.

"I do, but my life is here. St. Mary's is where your grandfather is buried and my parents. I'm not comfortable walking away from my past into an unknown future. That's for young people, not me." Granny rose and touched Emmie on the shoulder. "Look at me, please."

Emmie did as requested. When had her grandmother aged? Her hair held more white strands than brown, and her forehead had more furrows than Emmie remembered.

"I know how much you want to be with your mother and father. If you want to go, I'll write them tonight and get you a train ticket. I'd miss you, but keeping you here for my sake is wrong. You might be missing out on meeting your husband if you don't go."

"No. I'll not go. I promised to stay until you sell the house. When that happens, please say you'll come with me. Even if for a short visit. You could return if you don't like Kansas."

"I'll consider it, but this town has always been my home. I can't bear to leave it behind."

"I understand, but the family won't be complete until we're all together." She sat back in her chair and picked up the paring knife and a potato.

"Honey, we aren't now. Your grandfather isn't here, and the brothers you lost are in heaven. When we all get through those gates and see our Father's face, we will be together again, but not until that happens."

"I hope it's not for a long time. I want us to be a family here forever." She missed her mother and father so much she could weep. If only she hadn't promised her parents that she would help Granny with the boardinghouse until she sold it. "Let's not talk about this anymore. It makes me sad." She popped a thin potato slice into her mouth, enjoying the crunch but wishing she'd sprinkled it with salt first.

"Agreed. Now, remember that handsome young man that helped you at the wedding?"

Emmie's heart skipped.

"Well, seems Mr. Knipp needs a place to rest his head. He is our newest boarder. I let him the room for the same amount as Milton and Walter. He's trying to get his feet under him and looks like he hasn't slept in a week."

"Why would you do that? You don't charge those two hardly enough to cover their food. We agreed we wouldn't take any more boarders."

"I have my reasons, dear. This is still my boardinghouse, and besides, maybe God is nudging me to help that man. Or maybe He wants you to be in close proximity and generate some fondness for Landon."

Emmie touched her hair and found a loose strand. She tucked it behind her ear.

Granny laughed. "You'll have time to freshen up before he gets here for dinner."

"It doesn't matter. I'm not looking for a husband in this town, and I believe he intends to stay here a long time since he is opening a store." She rose and carried the bowl of peeled potatoes to the stove. "I'm going to pray for all the boarders to get married and for you to change your mind about Kansas." She hadn't counted on Mr. Knipp showing up. He could take care of finding his own wife.

She could only hope she was long gone when he did.

CHAPTER 6

Landon propped the broom handle against the wall. The surrounding air swirled and sparkled as sunlight hit the dust. He was grateful he remembered to tie a cloth around his head, cowboy style, covering his nose and mouth. Nothing could be done for his glasses. He slid them off and wiped them clean with a cloth he carried in his pocket, careful not to pull on the gold rims.

He surveyed his work. The broom bristles left streaks, but he didn't intend for the first round to be perfect. This building had been vacant for quite a while. It would take more turns around the floor with the broom, followed by a good mopping, to rid the place of the dust still circulating in the air. For now, this amount of cleaning would do.

He chose the nearest crate to unpack. He pried at the lid with a crowbar. It didn't budge. He took a deep breath and pushed. The nails gave way with a screech. As he pulled the lid away, the packing straw sprang to life and settled with a soft swish on the floor. He dug through, retrieving small bisque porcelain figurines from Germany. These would go into the case closest to the door. They would bring customers farther inside. Who could resist a girl holding a kitten?

He pushed the crate nearer to the case and removed the contents, placing the pretties, as his mother called them, on top. He arranged them by size, the smallest items on the top shelf. Or they would be as soon as he found the crate with the velvet he needed to line the shelves. Black fabric made the figurines look impressive, but not if it were covered in dust.

He pulled out his watch to check the time. He had precious little of it to spare. Snapping the cover of the watch closed, he trotted to the stairs where he'd left his packed valise. No time to brush the dust from his hair, or he would be late for dinner at the boardinghouse. He wanted to make a nice impression on the younger Miss Mueller. After all, he'd picked this town because of her.

He flew out the door, tripped on the stoop, and landed face-first in the street.

CHAPTER 7

If Emmie came to dinner dirty, then so be it. She wouldn't do more for Mr. Knipp than she did for the other men in the house, despite how handsome she found him back in July. Instead, pulling weeds from the garden would be a better use of her time. She yanked one. The root broke free, and she fell backward. She glanced around to see if anyone noticed. Walter and Milton were nowhere around. She relaxed her shoulders. This was not a tale she wanted retold over dinner tonight.

Back on her knees, she picked a few ripe tomatoes. She wiped the sweat from her brow and then collected some salad leaves for dinner. Did her parents have a garden? Probably not, as they would have arrived too late to put it in. Where were they getting their food? Did they have kindly neighbors who were sharing? She'd have to ask Granny if they could bring along the peaches they'd canned. They would be a special treat this winter.

Her grandmother's desire to stay in Trenton troubled Emmie's heart. Should she leave her or stay? Her father insisted that she stay until Granny was ready. But Granny would never leave Trenton willingly. "God, why can't our family be together? And what about Walter and Milton, Lord? Can you show me which women in town would like to be married to them? They are old as Moses, but they would make good companions for someone."

"Emmie!"

She jumped at her grandmother's shout. Had she been praying aloud again? And when did Walter and Milton come out in the yard? Had they overheard her? They sent nasty looks her way. She ducked her head and studied the ground.

"Coming, Granny." She stood and grabbed the handle of the garden basket filled with today's offerings. Agnes Gray recently lost her husband. She would do for one of them, but that still left her one.

CHAPTER 8

"ARE YOU OKAY, SIR?"

Fancy stitched boots stood mere inches from his face. "I'm okay." Landon pushed off the dirty sidewalk and stood. "Bruised pride is all."

"Are you sure? You took quite a tumble from what I saw." The man waited for an answer.

"I'm thankful it wasn't a customer that fell. I'll need to get that threshold fixed right away." He brushed off his pants and the front of his coat, pausing at the pocket. His spectacles. Had they survived the impact?

He retrieved them. And shook his head. "That's not good." The frames were bent and one lens cracked. "Do you know where I can get these repaired? And a good carpenter as well?"

"Sure do. Mr. Carr at the pharmacy can help you with those spectacles and ask for Terrance at the lumber yard. He'll get someone over here to fix your doorway tomorrow morning."

Landon offered a handshake. "I'm much obliged. I'm Landon Knipp."

"Clyde Myeberger. Glad to meet you. I'm down the street at the livery. If you need a horse, stop by."

"I will, and hope you return the favor when I open the store."

"What kind of wares are you offering here?"

"Knipp Emporium will be stocked with unusual and exotic items from around the world. Perfect for gift giving and decorating your home."

"My wife will be excited when she hears that. She misses the big stores in Saint Louis. We might have to trade you horse rentals for what she'll add to her account." Clyde slapped his leg and laughed. "Won't be the first store I've had to do that with. Where were you off to in such a hurry?"

"The boardinghouse. I'm staying there for a while. I'd better get there, or I'll miss dinner."

"You don't want that. Those women are known for their meals. I am surprised they took you on as a boarder. The young one has been telling everyone they're leaving for Kansas soon."

"Then I'm grateful for the chance." How could he keep Miss Emmie Mueller from leaving before he got her to fall in love with him?

—————

"Emmie, answer the door. That's got to be our new boarder." Granny drew her lips in a thin line. "And be nice."

"I will." Emmie untied her apron and laid it across the back of the kitchen chair. When she approached the screen door, she stifled a chuckle. Mr. Knipp looked nothing like her memory. Gone was the well-dressed gentleman. The man in his place wore dust in his hair and on his clothing.

"Difficult trip from town, Mr. Knipp?" She opened the door for him.

"Ah, it's you, and this time I didn't have to catch you." He rotated his hat in his hands.

Would he ever forget her clumsiness? Had he thought about her, too? The words in her mouth dried like glue, keeping her from speaking.

"Mr. Knipp, come in." Granny came up behind Emmie. "After today, you must think of this as your home. There'll be no need to knock."

"Move aside, Emmie. Let him pass through. Why don't you get the bread out of the oven, and I'll show him upstairs?" She nudged Emmie to the side. "This way, Mr. Knipp. You'll be staying in room seven at the top of the stairs on the left."

Mr. Knipp grabbed his valise. "Yes, ma'am."

Emmie blinked twice. That man with his dark brown eyes struck something deep inside of her. She didn't have a name for the warmth running through her. She felt her forehead. Maybe she'd spent too much time in the garden during the hottest part of the day. Yes, that must be the reason. A cup of water was all she needed. She scurried into the kitchen well aware of his pleasant scent.

Landon surveyed the room he'd be living in for a while. He dropped his valise by the armoire, intending to unpack later. He eyed the bed with delight. And sat on it. Soft and not a single creak or groan. Tonight, he would sleep well. The washstand had a pitcher of water, and the mirror alerted him that he needed to use that water. The dust from the shop must have resettled all over him. He glanced at his knees. They, too, were dirty from his fall. He brushed away the dirt.

At a knock on the door frame, Landon turned.

"Thought I'd introduce myself before dinner. Walter Hoffman. The other boarder is Milton Taylor."

He stood. "Landon Knipp."

"Planning on staying long?"

"At least six months, maybe a year. I'm opening Knipp Emporium and decided it would be easier if I didn't have to cook and clean on top of that."

Walter touched his finger to pursed lips and took one step back, looked both ways, and reentered the room.

How odd. Why was the man telling him to be quiet?

"Good, Miss Emmie is downstairs. You'll have to watch out for her."

"Why?" Had he made a mistake moving here? Was the woman out of her mind? Dangerous?

"Milton and me figured out what she's doing. She's trying to find wives for all of us."

"Why would she do that?"

"Once we move out, she and her grandmother can go to Kansas to be with the rest of the family. I don't think her grandmother wants to go."

Landon scratched his head. "I don't understand why you must marry for that to happen."

"Because Mrs. Mueller won't sell the house unless we have homes and someone to take care of us." Walter's face reddened. "She likes us. We like her. Why would we want to marry and leave her cooking? We have it good here. Getting hitched would be a lot of hard work. Wives need tending to, and they ask too much. Milton and I have always been bachelors, never envious of our friends who married."

Walter said something about checkers on the porch, but the words circulating in Landon's mind were about Emmie moving to Kansas. Foolish. That's what he'd been. He'd rushed to this town without asking God if Emmie was the one for him. After all, what did he even know about her except she was pretty?

CHAPTER 9

In the kitchen, Emmie fanned her face. Mr. Knipp must think her a fool. She'd talked to him twice before, but now, faced with him on her doorstep, all of her vocabulary dissolved like sugar in the rain. It was the dimple in his cheek. It had to be. Most of the men she knew had beards, but not Mr. Knipp. When he smiled at her, the evening sun highlighted that small indent, making him look most charming. She was getting heated again. Was she sick? She splashed a bit of cool water onto her face.

"Emmie, did you check the bread? I won't be serving burned food to anyone." Granny pushed past her and opened the oven. The heat blasted through the kitchen.

The oven, of course. That's why she was so warm. "Let me get that for you, while you refill the pitcher with tea."

"Don't be telling me how to run this kitchen, young'un. You only get to boss others when you have your own place."

"Granny! I wasn't!"

"Never mind. I'd rather do the tea than that hot oven anyway."

Emmie stared at her grandmother as she walked away. Was that the problem with moving? Did Granny worry about losing her place in the kitchen since they would all be in the same house?

Granny turned. "Get that bread on a plate and bring it in. The men are waiting."

"Yes, ma'am." Emmie filled the plate and then followed her grandmother into the dining room. She stopped so fast the bread came close to flying off onto the floor. No one was in the right spot.

Walter and Milton had moved from where they'd been sitting for five years. Walter slid out of his chair and took the tea pitcher from her grandmother and set it on the table.

"Mrs. Mueller, allow me." Walter yanked out an empty chair, and Granny slipped into it.

"Thank you."

Emmie stared at the arrangement. There was only one space left. Next to Landon. She took a step.

He hopped up and grabbed the bread plate from her and repeated the actions of Walter.

Walter and Milton sported wide grins. They were up to something.

The next morning, Landon smiled all the way to work. Miss Emmie Mueller had no idea the older gentlemen had figured out her plan, and it seemed they'd decided to match her with him. If they succeeded, the men would be able to stay unwed and waited upon by Emmie's grandmother.

A dog barked from behind a picket fence and startled him. Glad for the jolt of reality, he pushed Emmie from his mind and returned to his massive list of things to achieve at the emporium. Several townspeople nodded at him as he passed, and his spirit lightened. Today, he would visit the owner of the mercantile and assure him that their businesses would not compete for customers.

As he approached, he saw a youngster sitting on the stoop of his store. When he drew close, the boy jumped to his feet.

"Sir, do you have any work for me?"

The boy wore clean clothes and combed hair. Not small in stature. Muscular. "I might." Landon inserted the key into the lock and turned. It didn't budge.

"You have to rattle it inside the lock to make it work. Most of the stores on this street have the same problem."

Landon twisted the key back and forth, and the tumbler clicked. "Thank you for that tip. You're already proving your value. What's your name?"

"Duck."

"Duck?"

"That's what they call me. My real name is Cyrus."

Landon pushed the door open and motioned the boy to follow him. "How did you get that nickname?"

"My ma says I liked to say the word over and over when I was little, so they started calling me that because I would say it back and laugh."

"Interesting. Do you like being called that?" Landon grimaced at the dust-covered floor.

"I don't mind, but I'd like to be Cyrus when I get older. Probably won't happen as long as I live here. That's why I have to earn money so I can move away. I have five older brothers. They work for my dad. I could, too, but they won't let me do any of the fun stuff. I always have to clean the stalls, and they never call me Cyrus."

Landon understood Cyrus's place in life. "I think I'll call you by your given name. Then maybe others will follow. I, too, have older brothers, and it can be difficult to break their idea of who you are. They tend to think of you as the little brother forever. Do you mind if I call you Cyrus?"

"No, sir." He stood straighter. "Does that mean I get to work here?"

"You're the first to ask. When can you start?"

"Right now."

"Then let's open a few of these boxes and see what's inside."

Emmie carried a bucket with a scrub brush, rags, and Kirk's Castile soap. "Granny, I don't see why we need to help Mr. Knipp. He didn't ask us to." The wind whipped at her skirt hem.

"He's living with us, and he has no family nearby. It's the right thing to do." Granny tugged the basket she carried into the crook of her elbow.

They were almost at the store. It had been vacant for quite some time, and she imagined there would be plenty of dust and dead bugs to remove. "What if he doesn't want our help?"

"Then we will leave the cleaning tools if he needs them, along with these blueberry muffins."

"Maybe we'll get a peek at some of the specialty items he's planning to sell. Maybe we can buy a few things to take with us to Kansas."

"Your mother won't need any frippery on the prairie. You best save your egg money for winter boots, and a thicker coat." Granny took a ragged breath. "The wind is stirring up something. As sticky as the air is, maybe a storm."

Emmie's shoulders sagged. Granny was right. Pretty things were not needed out West. It might be better if she bought a shovel. Still, she wouldn't give up on the idea of something for her mother. Something that would survive the train trip, small enough that it wouldn't take precious space in her trunk, and something special to bring a smile to her mother's face. Her heart ached. She wanted to be with her family. She missed them so. Why did God continue to make it difficult to leave? She would have to pray harder.

CHAPTER 10

CRATE LIDS RESTED ON the floor. The door opened. Straw swirled and crept across the wood planks. "Sorry, we aren't open yet," Landon yelled.

"We aren't here to shop, Mr. Knipp. We came to help."

The sunlight behind Miss Emmie cast a golden glow around her. Stunned by the sight, Landon was rooted to the floor, searching for air.

Cyrus returned from the back room. "Mr. Knipp, I—"

"Duck, I didn't know you were working for Mr. Knipp." Granny held out her basket. "I brought muffins. Come get one."

Cyrus took a giant step, then stopped and looked at Landon for permission.

"Go ahead. We've decided to call him Cyrus from now on since that's his given name."

"That's a splendid idea. I'll try to remember to call you that." Emmie waded through the straw. "You have quite a mess here."

"We have, but it's better than it was." Landon shoved two empty crates to the center of the store. "It's not as nice as the boardinghouse, but please, have a seat."

"Nonsense." Granny put her basket on one of the crates. "Grab yourself a muffin, and Emmie and I will get to liberating this room of all that straw."

"You don't need to. That's my job." Cyrus scrunched his eyebrows.

"Humph. Duck, are you afraid if this gets done you won't have a job tomorrow?" Granny stared at him hard enough to make a grown man yell, "Uncle!"

"Yes, ma'am."

"Mr. Knipp, are you going to have more work for the boy, or is this it?"

Landon squirmed. He hadn't thought that far ahead. Once the store was clean and set up, would he need Cyrus? There were inventory sheets to be filled out, and he could use help for that. "Cyrus, I'll keep you on. I broke my glasses, and until they are repaired, I won't be able to do any of the paperwork."

Silence filled the room.

"Sir. I can't read or write." Cyrus stared at the floor.

"That's because you ducked out of school so much. Maybe that's why they call you Duck." Granny shook her head. "Regrets are hard to leave behind. Mr. Knipp, Emmie will help you with the books until you can see again."

"Granny!" Her face pinked.

"I'd be obliged, Miss Mueller, if you would help me." They would be together every day for at least a week. His heart quickened. Maybe he'd be able to find a way to make her stay in Trenton. He squeezed Cyrus's shoulder. "No excuses, Cyrus. If you want to be a man in this world, you need to learn to read and write. If you want, I can teach you."

"That's a nice offer," Emmie said. "Cyrus, you need to take this opportunity to learn. Mr. Knipp, I can see you're a kind soul." Her face pinked.

"Please understand. You won't be working for free. You'll be earning a wage."

Her eyes widened. "I'll come help you when Granny doesn't need me."

"I won't need you tomorrow." Mrs. Mueller nodded. "Yep, you two can walk here together in the morning. Now, I insist everyone grab a muffin. We've got some cleaning to do, and we might as well have happy stomachs while we do it."

Landon couldn't believe how fast the pieces of his life were falling together. Could this be God's plan despite his lack of prayer on the matter?

A week later, Emmie's neck and shoulders ached. She had no idea how much work it took to set up a store. Landon's spectacles hadn't arrived yet, so she spent hours printing merchandise names, the quantity, and the costs to buy and to sell. She picked up a figurine. Her mother would love this one of a woman surrounded by children. It was too heavy to take to Kansas. With a sigh, she held it high and slid it onto the display shelf.

Landon came up behind her, breathing hard. "I thought you were going to drop it, but I see you have very long arms."

Emmie nodded. Face burning and tears stinging, she couldn't speak. She whirled away from him and went back to the ledgers.

"Did you hurt yourself?"

"No, but I think you need to help Cyrus." His words scraped an old scar raw. She peeked between her eyelashes as he went to the end of the counter where Cyrus practiced writing his letters on the slate Landon provided. Watching Landon work with the boy filled her heart with feelings she didn't want. She couldn't get attached to him, no matter how much she thought he'd make a wonderful husband. Even if she was staying in Trenton, which she wasn't, he'd be just like all the other boys, now men, in this town. No one wanted Monkey Arms for a wife.

In fact, she needed to get back to her purpose. Finding wives for Milton and Walter. Working with Landon slowed down her progress. She'd eliminated the Geis sisters once she'd discovered they didn't eat pork after growing up on a pig farm. That would never work, not the way those two liked their bacon.

"Say the letter name as you write it, Cyrus. You know I can't see the board well, so Miss Emmie will check it later."

"I know my ABCs."

"Yes, but you can't write them, and that means you can't recognize them in words. Your choice. Do you want to be Cyrus or Duck?"

Emmie straightened at Landon's tough words. "Landon, do you think—"

"Miss Emmie, would you be so kind as to run to the pharmacy and see if my spectacles have arrived? Not being able to do half of my job is making me cranky."

She closed the ledger and set the pencil next to it. "Yes, of course, but that's no excuse for being mean to Cyrus."

"It's okay, Miss Emmie. I want to learn. Mr. Knipp is right. I mean, correct. I have to do the baby work if I want to be a learned man, like him."

Emmie smiled at the word change. Cyrus didn't realize he also received multiple vocabulary lessons when he worked with Landon. She slid her hat on her head and secured it with pins. "I'll be back shortly. Is there anything else I should get while I'm out?"

"Keep working, Cyrus." He walked over to Emmie and whispered in her ear. "Bring back some licorice whips, please. This boy deserves a reward."

The words tickled her ear. She shivered. Mercy, she needed to stop working here soon, or she'd be wanting to stay in Trenton. She took a step away. "Should I put everything on your account?"

"Yes, and take your time. I know how hard it is to write numbers all morning. Maybe this afternoon, we'll have a customer or two wander in."

"Don't fret. Tomorrow, everyone will be in town. Saturday is when people come from the small towns around us. You'll sell so much that an order will need to be placed on Monday. I'm sure of it." She picked up her reticule.

"I hope they do purchase, but most will be lookers."

"And there will be those that remember they want to return here when they have extra money. I'll pick up the lunch Granny promised while I'm out. Cyrus, there will be food for you, too, so don't go running off."

Emmie prayed her prediction of sales would be so as she left the store. Landon's store had beautiful things, but costly. Rugs from India, china from England, and parasols from France weren't everyday items. She'd love a lace parasol but couldn't see a use for it on a homestead in Kansas.

Landon checked his pocket watch. Emmie should be back by now. He peered out the door. No sign of her coming up the sidewalk. Quite unlike her. He stepped inside. He studied the merchandise displays and didn't see anything to change. He chose the right building. With the big display windows on the corner, his wares couldn't be ignored.

But why weren't the customers coming? His skin itched. He could almost feel the red welts popping up on his back. *Please, God, not hives. I'm stepping back. You are in control.*

Cyrus sat at a small table writing the alphabet. "I wish Miss Mueller would come. I'm hungry."

"Why don't you run down to the boardinghouse and help her carry back the basket. I'm sure she has a reason for being gone so long."

"Maybe she's waiting for a pie to cool." Cyrus licked his lips. "I hope it's a peach crumble. Those are the best." He pushed his slate and chalk to the corner of the table. "I'll be back soon."

Landon watched as Cyrus left, shirttail flying through the door after him.

"Sorry, ma'am."

Cyrus bumped into someone. Maybe a customer? Landon brushed the front of his coat and prepared to greet whoever entered.

A cloud moved, and the sunlight hit the door, blinding him as a woman entered. He squinted and took a step forward. "Welcome to Knipp Emporium."

"Landon?"

It was a voice he never expected to hear again, one that had smashed his dreams and destroyed a friendship. One he'd vowed to never again hear.

No. It couldn't be her.

Chapter 11

"Not now, Rooster." Emmie scooted away from the rooster attempting to snuggle with the hem of her skirt. She had Landon's spectacles in one hand and a letter from her mother in the other. Rooster would have to wait. "I'll bring you some corn when I leave." She bolted through the screen door, letting it bang behind her. Granny and Walter sat at the table slicing peaches.

Walter pushed back the chair and popped up.

"Emmie, you know better than that. I've taught you not to let the door slam." Granny's face held a tinge of pink.

What did that mean?

"I think I'll see if Milton feels like a game of checkers." Walter sped past Emmie.

"I'm sorry. I stopped at the post office, and there is a letter from Momma. I rushed home so we could read it together." She set her reticule and Landon's glasses on the table.

"Looks like Landon's eyesight is not as important to you."

"No, not now. He's gone two weeks without them and a few more minutes won't matter. We have a letter from the family." She handed the envelope to her grandmother. "Hurry, open it and see what it says."

"Not so fast, missy. Things like this must be savored. How about you pour us a glass of tea? Then, we'll go sit on the porch, and see what's happening in the great state of Kansas. Though, it might be even more exciting to make you run back to town and give Landon his spectacles first." Granny set her knife next to the bowl.

"No, please don't. He'll be all right. Cyrus is there, and not one soul has come into the store today." She folded her hands together in a prayer position. "Please, don't make me wait."

"All right. Get the tea."

Emmie, holding the tall glasses, followed Granny through the front door and set them on the small wicker table between two rockers. Her heart raced. Would her mother have good news?

Granny settled in her chair. "Stop fidgeting and sit down."

She doubted that would stop her toes from tapping, but she did as ordered.

Granny ripped the end of the envelope with care and pulled out the paper. She unfolded it, then smoothed it against her apron and read aloud.

Dear Mama and Emmie,

We all miss you! Living in the city at first was entertaining, but the fun ran out. Knowing I wouldn't be living here, I haven't made close friends. I miss those I have in Trenton more than I thought. Postage money for letters must be used to purchase other items. Please tell Mrs. Diekman that I haven't forgotten about her and will write.

Robert has been working hard to prepare a place for us, and we'll be moved in by the time this letter reaches you. We're hoping our letters cross in the mail, and you have sold the boardinghouse by now. It would be best if you could be here before September to enjoy some of the fall season before winter arrives.

Emmie, there is little room to store clothing, so please give away some of yours. Anything you wear for social occasions won't be needed here. Mama, there is no need to bring all your aprons. Two would be best.

Father says he thinks he has found a good man for Emmie to marry but will respect her decision after they meet. He has the adjoining farm. He is a widower and has six children that need a mother. It would be best, Emmie, if you found you could look upon him with favor as we have so little room, and it is time you were married. You'd make a good mother.

⸱⸱⸱ℓℓ⸱⸱⸱

Six children. The words repeated themselves as Emmie walked back to the store. Was that the life she wanted? It certainly wasn't the one she'd been working on so hard to achieve. In her dream, the family would be together, planting crops and building their house. Marriage, yes, but not right away. Mother's letter made it sound like the minute she put foot on Kansas soil, she'd be whisked off to the church and back home in time to make dinner for six children and a husband. Did he have a home big enough to hold her clothing if she brought it?

"Miss Mueller."

Emmie stopped mere inches in front of Alma Pickens.

"Is everything all right?" Alma arched her eyebrow.

"Yes, I'm sorry I almost knocked you down. We had a letter from Mother. . ." Alma had married a man with children and, as far as Emmie knew, she loved being their mother. Maybe this was God's way of telling her not to worry.

"Is everything okay with them? Roy and I were surprised to hear they'd left to start over in Kansas."

"Yes, they're fine. Mother misses her friends, of course. There is no stopping my father when he decides to do something. This time, he said Trenton had grown too big. He wanted to walk miles before seeing anyone."

"How sad for your mother, she being sociable and all."

Mother must be lonely. She'd always enjoyed her friendships and knowing almost everyone in town. So did Emmie. Moving to Kansas appealed to her far less today than ever. "Have you been to the Knipp Emporium yet?"

"No, I heard it has unusual items for sale."

"Our newest boarder owns the store. You would like it. Why—"

"Miss Mueller!"

Cyrus ran up to them. "There you are. Do you have pie? Is that why you're late with our lunch?"

Emmie laughed. "No, no pie today, but I'll bring some tomorrow. Why don't you take the basket and head to the store?

"Cyrus?" Anna looked closer. "Isn't your name Duck?"

"No, ma'am. And now Mr. Knipp says people need to start calling me by my real name. And that's Cyrus." He took the basket. "I need to get back. A customer came in when I came out the door. I hope it's not to complain because I almost knocked her over."

"Go, then. Hurry up and tell Mr. Knipp I'll be along in a little while." He ran off. The milk in the jars might turn to butter the way the basket bobbed in his hand.

"Mr. Knipp must be a good influence on the boy. I'm glad he's using his name. It always felt odd calling him Duck."

"Mr. Knipp is teaching him to read as well. Why don't you walk to the store with me? I have some questions, if you don't mind answering."

"I'm on my way to my father's, but I'll pop in soon when Roy is with me. What do you have on your mind?"

"What's it like to take care of children when you've never had any? My mother has a husband picked out for me. He is a widower with six kids. I don't even know his name. Mother didn't think to include it." Emmie couldn't swallow. A new home in a new state and now, marriage. "I don't know what to do."

"Julia?" Landon forced her name past his lips. "What are you doing here? Did Harry send you?"

"I had to get away for a while. I saw your mother at church, and she told me about this town, that you liked it." She did a slow turn. "It's not as big as your father's store, but I like it. Simple surroundings for extravagant things."

"But, why come here?" His mind processed thoughts like boots wading through the mud. The woman he once loved now stood in his store wearing black. Black. Gone were the colorful satins she'd preferred. "Julia? Harry?"

"He passed a month ago. I thought your mother would have let you know."

Her words punched his lungs. His breath escaped. Harry, his best friend until he'd stolen Julia from him, now gone. "What—what happened?"

"Runaway carriage. Please, I don't want to talk about it. I'm lost without him. I'm sorry, I know that hurts you, but he was my everything." She sniffed.

Landon pulled a handkerchief from his pocket. "Here."

She took it and wiped tears from her eyes. "I know you're angry, and you don't want to see me. I had to go somewhere. I knew if I came here, I could be assured to know one person that I could trust if I needed help. I knew you would look after me."

"Julia—"

"Only as a good friend, Landon. My heart still wants Harry."

Her eyes filled with tears and snared him. He would take care of her. He wished he hadn't been so angry with Harry.

He thought there would be time once he had a wife of his own for him and Harry to be friends again.

"Where are you staying?"

"I checked in at White Hotel yesterday, but it's lonely eating by myself, strangers giving me sideways glances and wondering where I came from. And saying how sad it is that I'm a widow."

Feelings he thought dead now sparked. Should he fan them? They had a history together. She'd always hated that he traveled, but maybe now that he was staying in one place? But what about Emmie? Her sunny smile tugged at his heart.

CHAPTER 12

EMMIE ROLLED ALMA'S ADVICE around in her thoughts. Alma insisted on Roy courting her before they married, despite the attempt of her father to have them marry within days of meeting each other. Could she do the same? Months ago, she might have thought it possible. Then Landon arrived.

Confused by her feelings, Emmie stepped inside the mercantile to purchase the licorice whips he'd requested. In her excitement about the letter, she'd forgotten to buy them. Landon's kindness to Cyrus touched her heart.

What would Kansas be like? Would she be able to shop as she did here? She would miss this store and the family who ran it. She gazed at the shelves. How long would she be able to remember the coolness of this store after she left? It didn't seem important compared to being with her family, but as the weeks crept by, she noticed the small things she'd taken for granted forever. Her friends, of course. Then there were the townspeople, like Mr. Rutherford at the post office. And did they have a confectioner store where she was going?

"Afternoon, Miss Mueller. Have you heard from your parents?" Widow Beckett held a basket.

"We had a letter today. Mother is missing her friends."

"As we miss her, too."

Widow Beckett's sparkling eyes caught her attention. Didn't she have a sister? "Why don't you come for dinner tomorrow evening? Ask your sister, too. Granny would love to share what she knows with you."

"I'm sure Dorthea would enjoy getting out. We're both so set in our ways that we've become quite boring." Widow Beckett smiled and straightened her posture. "Can we bring something? I've picked up some cornstarch to make a pie. I wouldn't mind sharing it."

"Granny will be thrilled to have company and insulted if you bring a dish. I know she's working on peaches today, so there will be an abundance of peach pie tomorrow. I'll see you then." At least Emmie hoped her grandmother would approve. She'd forgotten about these two older women. Sisters. Perfect for Walter and Milton. She almost skipped to the counter where the licorice whips tempted the little children from their glass jar. But once she found brides she could leave town.

Leave Landon.

———

Landon battled back his feelings of attraction for Julia. Grasping for the reasons she'd chosen his best friend over him. Despite her saying she couldn't get past her grief, he was dubious. There wasn't a real reason for her to come to Trenton. She had relatives in many places across the country. In fact, her sister lived in Collinsville.

He backed away from her as Cyrus tromped through the door. "No, pie today, but Mrs. Mueller will make some for tomorrow. Miss Emmie sent me on without her. She's yacking with Mrs. Pickens."

"Whoa, Cyrus. We have a customer."

"S–Sorry, sir." Cyrus set the basket on the floor. "Welcome to Knipp Emporium. Can I show you our newest selection of gloves?"

"Thank you, but I've seen the store and not found what I've wanted." She gave him a sour-grape frown.

"Mr. Knipp says we can order anything. Would you like me to get you a catalog?"

Landon choked back laughter while watching Cyrus's salesmanship.

"Again, thank you. You're a bit young to work the sales floor, aren't you?"

"No, ma'am. Mr. Knipp is teaching me how to run a store."

Julia turned toward Landon. "I thought you didn't like children." She shrugged. "I'll be off. Maybe you can meet me for dinner this week?"

"He can't. He has to eat at Mueller's boardinghouse every day because that's where he lives and his meals are included." Cyrus grasped the basket handle. "We even get our lunch from there. If you're leaving then, we can eat it, right, Mr. Knipp? Because we don't eat in front of customers."

"That is store policy." He could change it, of course, but seeing Julia left his mind in a jumble. "Let me escort you to the door."

"Come back anytime. We'll have new things arriving daily." Cyrus set the basket on the counter and emptied it.

━ℓℓℓ━

Emmie blinked in the bright sunlight. Then blinked again. Landon stood outside the emporium with a woman dressed in black. The woman moved her hands fast enough to stir up a breeze. Why did she stand so close to Landon? Who was she?

He bent down close to her. Emmie held her breath. He was close enough to kiss her. Did he know her? She strangled the licorice whips in her hand. Cyrus would want them, but Emmie couldn't get her feet to move forward. Why was she upset? She knew nothing about this woman. Except that the woman didn't mind when Landon touched her arm. She couldn't explain why that bothered her, but it did.

Heartsick, she turned and went back into the mercantile. She'd wait until the woman left to take Cyrus his treat. Then she was going home, because Granny could use her. There were floors to scrub and dusty front windows to wash. Yes, she'd been spending far too much time with Landon.

Chapter 13

"Emmie, this was not a good day to invite the Widow Beckett and her sister to dinner. I wanted to get the sheets washed. And you promised Cyrus peach pie. Why didn't you invite him to dinner, too?" Granny measured the flour and plopped it into the bowl. "Hand me the vinegar."

"Yes, ma'am." Emmie racked her brain. She would have to help Granny today if the plan was going to work. "We can do it together. I'll strip the sheets and wash them. You work on the pie, because you make the best in the county. Anyone can wash up sheets."

"Stop trying to butter me up. Hurry upstairs then and get to work. Walter and Milton went for a walk. You know how they like to inspect the town in the morning. The old fools. Don't know what they expect to find out of place."

"At least it gives us a chance to tidy." Emmie bounded up the steps. In no time, she had the sheets off of Milton and Walter's beds. She wanted to be done before they returned, otherwise she'd have to listen to multiple stories of their youth. She paused at the entrance to Landon's room. It smelled different. Much nicer than the older men's rooms. Intoxicating with the scent he wore. She took a deep breath. What would it feel like to be in his arms?

If she was affected this deeply by Landon's cologne, she would get some for the bachelors. It wouldn't hurt their chances of attracting Widow Beckett and her sister's attention. But what did he use? She couldn't ask him. She moved to the dresser to search for the bottle. Once she knew the name, she could purchase it.

His carpetbag sat unpacked on the dresser, his shaving items next to it. She reached for a bottle and brushed the side of the luggage. It crashed to the floor. Horror flooded through her. Once again Monkey Arms flew forefront in her mind.

She knelt to repack the items that spilled from the valise. She grabbed a picture frame. Maybe it was a photo of Landon's family. She flipped it over. Instead, it was the woman at the store. She pushed it to the bottom of the bag along with a few other things, set the bag on the dresser, and then yanked off the bed sheets hard enough to tear them.

***

"Miss Emmie, what's got you so excitable this evening?" Milton drew his eyebrows together into one long brow.

"I enjoy having guests for dinner, don't you?" Emmie placed the fork and knife on the table. She stood back. "It looks nice, doesn't it?"

Walter nudged Milton. "Who did you invite?"

"The Widow Beckett and her sister. I ran into the Widow Beckett yesterday, and she seemed so sad. I thought an evening dinner with all of us would cheer her." She turned away so they wouldn't see her face. She might give her plan away.

"Milton, it's going to be a long night. Miss Emmie, we like it when it's just us around the table. There's no need to put on our best behavior." Walter sighed.

"It's good for both of you to keep those skills your mothers taught you." The front door opened. Good, Landon had returned. He could help her with these two. They could learn quite a bit from him.

"Emmie, I hope you don't mind, but I brought along a friend."

The woman in the photograph stood in the doorway. Emmie forced a smile. "Of course not. Granny always says the boarders should treat this home like their own."

"Thank you. This is Mrs. Julia Crump. Julia, this is Miss Emmie Mueller."

"Pleased to meet you, Emmie."

The use of her first name took Emmie aback. Did the woman think she was a servant? "Please, take her to the dining room, Mr. Knipp. We'll be serving as soon as the others arrive."

Landon had noticed the way Emmie had turned frosty when Julia wrapped her arm through his as if she belonged to him. He wanted to refuse to bring Julia to the boardinghouse, but she'd been waiting on the boardwalk when he locked the shop door.

There was no time to explain before Emmie ushered them into the dining room.

"Who's this?" Walter scrunched his face. "It's not the sisters we were expecting. Milton fetch a chair from the kitchen."

Milton nodded and in his ghostlike way disappeared through the door. Come to think of it, that man didn't speak much ever. Landon introduced Julia to Walter. "What sisters are coming?"

"Miss Emmie invited some from the church. I imagine—"

Emmie stepped into the room. "What do you imagine, Walter?"

"Thinking about dinner. When are we going to eat?"

"Don't be such a curmudgeon. We have guests tonight." There was a soft knock on the door. "And there are the rest of dinner guests. I'll let them in and, Walter, behave. Where is Milton?"

"He went for another chair. If he was smart, he kept on going out the door."

"Walter!"

"I apologize, Miss Emmie. I'll let the women in and get everyone seated while you help your grandmother."

"Thank you." Emmie hurried toward the kitchen. Granny would not be happy about having another guest at the table tonight.

"Another person?" Granny grabbed Milton's arm before he took the chair from the kitchen. "Get that in there and come back for another place setting. Tonight, you are family, and family helps out."

"Yes, yes, ma'am." Milton's face reddened as he rushed from the room.

Granny rested her hands on her cheeks. "I'm getting too old for this kind of entertaining."

"Nonsense." Walter entered the kitchen with Milton shadowing him. "Let's start carrying out the food."

"Bless you, men. I never thought I'd let that happen in my house, but today I'm grateful for the help."

Emmie shrunk into the corner. Why hadn't she considered how much work this would be for Granny? She was old and tired. All the more reason to move to Kansas with the family once she got Milton and Walter married, if she could get Granny to go.

Following her grandmother to the dining room with the bowl of peas, she almost dropped it when she saw the seating arrangement. Milton or Walter, probably the latter, had put all the women on one side of the table and the men on the other. And somehow, he'd managed to put Julia in front of Milton, leaving empty seats in front of himself and Landon. Before she could move, her grandmother slid into the chair across from Walter.

Somewhat befuddled, Emmie sat, trying to corral her thoughts as to how this happened before Walter quit blessing the food.

CHAPTER 14

"Miss Emmie, could you run over to Knipp's and pick up some of that nice-smelling hair stuff he has?" Walter stepped off the last step and groaned. "I'd go, but my feet are hurting today. It'll do me good to sit on the porch for a spell."

"Why didn't you ask Landon to bring some home for you tonight? I planned on staying home to help Granny." And every day after. Last night embarrassed her. Those rascals stole her plan and twisted it. Neither of them said more than two words to the sisters. They might as well have put their faces on their plates. Once the prayer was said, they remained silent for the meal except for the occasional, "Pass me some more potatoes."

And Landon. Why had he brought Julia? He didn't talk to her either. The only conversations taking place had been among the women. By the time dessert was served, Emmie and Granny were sniping at each other.

"I didn't think about it. There was so much noise from all of you women talking I couldn't think, much less come up with a question. And I didn't see him this morning at breakfast. So are you going?" He took a step on the porch and winced.

The poor man really did hurt, and besides, if they smelled as good as Landon, it would be easier for women to fall in love with them. "I'll let Granny know, and then I'll be off. But next time, try to ask Landon when he is here." She hadn't seen Landon either. He must have awakened early and gone in to the store.

By the time she arrived at the store, she had steeled herself against seeing Julia. The woman probably even wore Emmie's apron while she worked. She should be happy for Landon, but she wasn't. She couldn't come up with a single reason that he should marry Julia. She'd tried. Yes, she did. All night. And not one thing felt right about those two being together.

She stepped inside.

"Miss Emmie! You're late. Did you bring muffins or something?" Cyrus trotted across the floor and skidded to a stop. "You don't have a basket."

"I'm sorry. I'm on an errand for Mr. Hoffman, or I wouldn't be here."

"But you have to be. Mr. Knipp is having a terrible time with those numbers today. He can't even help me with my studies."

"What do you mean?" She glanced around the room. Landon stood in the darkest corner, covering his eyes. "Landon, what's wrong?" Her skirt swished across the floor as she rushed to him.

"The spectacles are the wrong strength. My eyes feel like they've been scratched by a cat. I came back last night and worked on the books too long. Then this morning, I couldn't stand to be in the light."

"You stayed here all night?"

"Yes. I walked Julia back to the hotel and then came here. It seemed too late to return to the boardinghouse. I didn't want to wake anyone."

"You have a key, and Walter and Milton can sleep through anything. Where did you sleep? On the floor?"

"There's an old bed upstairs, and I slept there, or rather tried to."

"You need some cold compresses on those eyes. Cyrus, run to the café and get a few ice chips." She opened the drawer with the delicate handkerchiefs and took out two.

"What are you doing?" Landon stared at her through his fingers.

"Making you feel better. When Cyrus gets back with the ice, I'll wrap the pieces in these, and you can put them over your eyes."

"But those are costly."

"You only get one set of eyes. Where's Julia this morning?"

"At her hotel, I suppose. Why?"

"I thought she would be working with you."

"No, I would never allow her behind the counter at my store."

That stung. Landon thought more highly of Julia. She pushed the handkerchiefs into his hands. "When Cyrus gets back, put the ice in them and hold them on your eyes. I'm going home."

—ell—

"Emmie?" Landon squinted. The film in his eyes moved, and he caught sight of her fleeing the store. "What just happened?"

Cyrus burst into the shop with earth-pounding steps. "Boy, oh boy, Miss Emmie sure seems all fired up about something. She was racing down the street. I bet she gets in trouble from Mrs. Mueller for walking fast. Why is she mad anyway?"

"I don't know. Women puzzle me."

"Did you poke her in the back? They don't seem to like that much." Cyrus handed Landon a cup with ice chunks in it. "Did you call her Monkey Arms? My brother told me they called her that at school. Made her really mad."

"No, of course, I didn't. Why would they do that, any-way?"

"My brother said she was always knocking things over with her arms. He said they should never have called her that. It wasn't a nice thing to do."

"He's right. And, no, I didn't call her any names." But he had mentioned her long arms earlier in the week. She hadn't reacted well to that. Now he understood why.

"I have to take the cup back right away. They only let me take it because they said they knew you would return it. How'd you get people to respect you like that?"

Landon folded the ice into the expensive handkerchiefs. He couldn't sell them now. "Time, Cyrus. Being true to your word is the best way to earn respect. If you say you're going to do something, then that's what you do.

"Even if you don't want to?"

"Sometimes." His stomach curled as he remembered a promise to Harry they'd made as kids to always be family. Harry broke the promise first. So did that let him out of fulfilling his side? Did he have to take care of Julia?

~ele~

Emmie couldn't wait to get home. In fact, if she could, she'd start packing her bags and hop on the train for Kansas tomorrow. Julia was too good, too sweet, too special to work at the store, but not Emmie. No, with her monkey arms, she was perfect to work behind the counter. Didn't even need a step stool or a ladder.

Walter and her grandmother were in the kitchen.

"Did you get it?" Walter took a step back from the counter where he'd been stealing a cookie.

"No. I didn't. You'll have to ask Landon tonight."

"What's wrong, Emmie? Are you coming down with something? Come over here. You look flushed." Granny settled her palm against Emmie's forehead.

Granny's touch felt cool and comforting. She would love to cuddle up on her lap and tell her how she felt about

Landon, and how he had made her feel today. But Walter hovered nearby, dropping crumbs on the floor. And besides, she was too big to get comfort from her grandmother's lap. After all, she was the one supposed to take care of Granny, not the other way around.

"Nothing is wrong." At least nothing Granny could fix. She was more determined than ever to find a match for Walter and Milton by the end of the week. Maybe the man that waited in Kansas with his six children wouldn't mind the way she looked.

"I'm glad you're back from the store. I felt so bad about Julia living at the hotel that I sent Milton to tell her there is a room for her here. You'll have to pack your things up and move in with me. She'll only be here for a little while, but a grieving woman should be surrounded by people who care for her."

Emmie choked back furious words. How could Granny ask the beautiful, most perfect Julia to move in? Now Emmie would be faced with watching Landon and Julia make butterfly eyes over breakfast and dinner every day.

The situation was now intolerable.

Chapter 15

HEAVYHEARTED, LANDON WENT THROUGH the motions of helping Cyrus recite his sums. Was it his place to take care of his best friend's wife? Julia was becoming a thorn in his side.

The day he caught Emmie on the church steps anything he might have felt for Julia evaporated. He and Julia were never meant to be together, and he wished he would've learned that before his friend passed away. He would tell her today to return to St. Louis or go to her family in Collinsville.

"Mr. Knipp, I'm going to promise you that I will learn my sums by this time next week." Cyrus, with his big brown eyes, looked at Landon intently. "Do you think I can do it?"

"I believe in you, Cyrus. This time next week, you will be proficient in your sums, and then we can start with subtraction."

Cyrus sighed.

"Buck up. You didn't think you could do this, and sub-traction will be easy now that you know addition. It's just doing the math backwards."

The bell on the door jangled. Landon looked up. A woman customer. His heart beat faster. "Welcome to Knipp Emporium. Please feel free to look around, or if you're looking for something special, I will be happy to assist you."

"Thank you. My husband will be here in a moment. I wanted to take a few moments to survey your wares. Miss Mueller told me I would enjoy this store. She made it sound so exciting that I had to come and check it out for myself. Is she here today?"

"She left early." And the way she left, he wasn't sure she would be back. He wished Cyrus were older, then he could be left alone with the store. He'd like to find Emmie and figure out what he'd done wrong.

"Mrs. Pickens likes to paint, mostly kittens, Mr. Knipp."

"Cyrus, I didn't see you back there." Mrs. Gibbons ran her hand over a silk wrap that lay on the counter.

"You remembered!" Cyrus's wide toothy grin touched Landon. If he accomplished nothing else in this town, he could be proud of helping this boy.

"I did. How about you show me something you think I would like to see."

Cyrus hustled around the counter. "We have some very nice china cups with drawings of birds, ma'am. Perhaps those would interest you, as we don't have any with kit-tens?"

Landon held back a laugh. Cyrus was a natural-born salesman.

———

Emmie's stomach hurt, but it did no good complaining to Granny, who'd sent her right back to the emporium. The last thing she wanted to do was cross that threshold. But facing her grandmother's wrath? Now that was something she wasn't willing to do.

"Emmie, you are here. Mr. Knipp told me you left for the day."

Alma. *Thank You, God, for sending this sweet person here today.* It was just what she needed. "I had to come back. I'd forgotten to pick up something for one of the boarders. What do you think of the store?"

"It's amazing. I found at least a dozen things I'd like to get for the girls. Roy will have something to say about that. I'm afraid I'll be baking a mess of pies to make him forget about the purchases."

Emmie gulped. She hadn't considered the fights married people sometimes had. "Does he get rough with you, Alma?" She lowered her voice. "Just tell me and you can live with us, or maybe you can go back to your father's house?"

Alma giggled. "No. Roy doesn't know how to be mean. He does, however, seem to have a different idea about what is essential for little girls."

"Miss Emmie, I showed Alma the painted bird cups. She's thinking about those. Should I put them on the counter just in case she quits thinking?" Cyrus finger-combed his slicked-down hair.

"That would be nice. Then she won't have to go looking for them again."

He crept across the floor with the two cups.

"I think he's afraid he might break them." Landon spoke behind Emmie. "Please don't feel you must buy them. It gives him a chance to practice his store behavior.

Where had he come from? The heat from his breath blew against her shoulder, right through her blouse. It warmed her from the inside. She forced herself to move away from him. "Have you met Mrs. Pickens?"

"I have. You have a delightful friend. I believe I'll help Cyrus. It seems he doesn't quite understand the concept of thinking about a purchase, as he is wrapping the cups."

Emmie pressed her palm over her heart as he walked away.

Alma touched her arm. "I think you best forget about that man in Kansas, Emmie. Someone else has claimed your heart."

Could Alma be right? Had Emmie given Landon her heart? What would it be like to call him husband? To make him breakfast and to have his children? Her heart galloped. She fanned herself.

"Are you hot, Miss Emmie?" Cyrus asked. "'Cause I sure am. My friends are going to the pond after lunch to fish and swim."

"Mr. Knipp, did you hear that? Cyrus is giving up his afternoon with friends to work. That's a very grown-up thing to do."

Cyrus cast his eyes to the slate full of math problems.

"Perhaps he should take some time to be a boy today. Do you think you can help me the rest of the afternoon, Emmie?"

Cyrus jumped off the stool. "Could you, Miss Emmie? Please? I've been working so hard, and before you know it, winter will be here."

Emmie laughed. "I'm sure I can handle working here while you have fun. But if you catch a mess of fish, would you bring some to the boardinghouse? Granny would delight in fresh fish for dinner. Come to think of it, we don't have anyone to fish for us anymore."

"You could fish if you wanted to."

"I could, but it wouldn't be proper, and you know it. Will you do it?"

"Yes, ma'am. I hope I catch some, but it's hot and sunny and well, you know fish. They don't like to be caught this time of day." His eyes widened. "I mean, some do like to snag the hook."

"Go on with you." Landon shook his head. "You see where those words took you, correct? You almost talked your way out of being able to go. Run along, and have a good swim."

"Thank you." Cyrus put his slate and chalk behind the counter. "See you tomorrow."

A hush fell over the store. Cyrus took up a great deal of space with his active body and general noise. Now she could hear Landon's every movement.

"Emmie, do you like working here?" He strolled over and leaned against the counter.

"Yes, I do. I'll miss it when I'm in Kansas. I've never had so much money of my own, except for the egg money, but that's never much." He was so close she could count his thick fringed eyelashes.

"What are you going to do with it?" He reached for the ledger resting on the counter and brushed against her hand.

Heat leaped from his hand to hers. She ached, wanting more of his touch. "Buy some warm clothes good for working on a farm, I suppose." The words clunked in her mouth. She didn't want to spend money on those items. No, farming didn't appeal to her. She liked being surrounded by the beautiful things in Landon's store. If she purchased the blue silk and made a dress, would Landon notice her as much as she did him?

CHAPTER 16

Emmie followed the breeze beckoning from her bedroom window. She'd packed her things and would take them into Granny's room in a moment. This might be the last time she would call this room her own. She plunked down on the window seat where she'd spent time talking to God and reading. A puff of wind graced her like a kiss. Voices floated through the window. She peered out. Landon stood on the front walk, close to Julia. They leaned in to each other, talking.

He pulled something out of his pocket and gave it to her. That's when Emmie knew it was over. She hadn't even had a chance with Landon, and until today, she hadn't known how much she wanted one.

She ought to look away but couldn't. When Landon reached out and wiped something from Julia's face, his hand stilled against her cheek. Julia reached her arms around him, and he followed suit, hugging her back.

Emmie's heart shattered. She flung herself on what used to be her bed and stared at the crack in the ceiling. Days ago, she wondered how long she would remember this room, and now all she wanted to do was forget it.

She wanted out of this town. Maybe she would go to Kansas alone. It was obvious to her that Granny's beloved boarders meant more to her than her own family.

"Landon, I'm sorry I rushed here expecting you to save me." Julia fingered the golden locket. "This is so special."

"It's all right. I thought you might like a photo of Harry, and I had one. We promised to look after each other's families when we were younger. While you and I were once close, it was more of a brother and sister relationship. At least on your part."

Her sorrow-filled eyes shimmered.

"I meant that it was better for you to marry Harry. It may have been a short marriage, but I heard from my family you were happy."

"We were, and Harry didn't run all over the world to avoid his family. That's where you and I fell apart."

"Maybe we should thank God He intervened. I wasn't ready to settle down. I had to do some growing up before moving back. Even now I've managed to put the Mississippi between my brothers and me."

"You had to. They were never going to let the youngest son be more important than them. What do they think of you opening a store here?"

"There's been some grumbling and mention of one of them taking it away from me if I fail."

"You won't. Harry always said you were the best of the Knipp brothers."

His heart warmed. "Harry was a good friend. He would want you to marry again."

She offered a weak smile. "Maybe someday, but I'm not ready yet. I thought I would be if it was you, but to be honest, I would have been miserable pining for Harry. What about you and Emmie? I've seen how you look at her."

"I'm hoping to convince her to stay here and not run off to Kansas."

"What if she won't?"

Landon's throat constricted. What if she didn't choose him? Twice rejected, he'd die a lonely man before he took another look at a woman.

"Emmie, can we take a walk after dinner?" Landon took the serving tray from her. He'd been waiting for her, for the chance to talk to her alone.

"I don't think so. Granny will need help cleaning up."

Milton appeared behind Emmie. He winked at Landon. "Walter and I will help her."

"But you've never—"

"It's about time we stopped be so lazy around here. You and your grandmother have been kind to treat us so well. So take the evening stroll with your fellow."

"He's not my—"

"I'll let Walter know." Milton left before Emmie could finish her sentence.

Landon straightened. He had the men on his side. Now, all he had to do was convince this blond beauty to stay in Trenton and marry him. Or for tonight, take a walk with him.

"What about Julia? Shouldn't you be asking her?" Her lips tightened into a straight line, and she looked away from him.

"It will be fine. I don't desire her presence with us for this conversation."

"Come on and sit down." Mrs. Mueller brushed past them with a plate of rolls.

"Yes, Granny. We'll be right there." Emmie turned to Landon. "I'll go with you, but only if you tell Julia at dinner that we're going for a walk."

"I will, and I promise it won't be a problem for her."

Chapter 17

The warm golden glow of the sun setting spread over the town and Emmie, making both stunning to Landon. Emmie was already beautiful, and downright angelic in the sunset colors.

"Does this walk have a purpose, Landon?"

"Yes. There is a house I discovered on the way to the store that I'm considering purchasing, and I wanted to know what you thought of it."

She shot him a quizzical glance.

"You've lived here all of your life, and I thought you could tell me the history of the place." And he wanted her reaction to it before he made an offer. It wouldn't do if she hated it.

"I can try to be helpful. Even though I have lived here a long time, I don't know everything about this town."

Landon stopped in front of the Victorian house that he wanted. The place with its green, rose, and blue painted accents struck him as happy. "This is it. I like the big porch, but it needs a swing and a few rocking chairs like you have at the boardinghouse. What do you think?"

"In primary school, I had a friend who lived here. One day, I spent the afternoon with her. It's a splendid house with a lot of rooms. I don't remember many details about the inside. I do know there is a large pantry because we played hide-and-seek and I hid in it."

"When did they move?"

"It was the oddest thing. One day she was at school and the next day she wasn't. Overnight they moved, and no one knew where they went. After that, a lot of people have lived here. There are rumors of it being haunted."

"Do you believe that?" This was something he didn't expect from her.

"No. I do believe in houses where windowpanes are not glazed properly, and the wind is able to send sounds through the cracks. That's probably what happened here a few times."

"That's something I'll check before making an offer."

"Why do you need such a big house to begin with? Most of my friends who are married start with smaller houses."

"I have no intention of ever moving. My parents lived in the house I grew up in since they were married. It's a great tradition to carry on. Putting down roots in this town is important to me."

"Why? When so many leave the places they were raised, why would you want to stay?"

"The world is not as exciting as one would think. I traveled all over while purchasing items for my father's store. I missed home. Because of that, I decided I would marry, stay in one town, and have a large family. That's why I need a big house, so everyone will be comfortable."

"But you don't even have a wife—"

"Not yet. But I soon will. That is if she will have me." He moved closer to her and touched her arm.

Emmie's bottom lip trembled, her eyes watered. She broke away from him. "I need to get back. They're lighting the lamps and Granny will need me." She took off at a fast clip.

"Wait up. Do you think the house will work?" He scurried to catch up. He'd done something wrong. Again.

"I'm sure you and your new bride will be happy in the house."

——ele——

It's not fair, God. Why did Landon have to have such lovely brown eyes? When had Emmie fallen so deeply in love with him? And now she couldn't have him. Julia would live in that wonderful house while Emmie settled in Kansas with the no-name farmer and his children.

She rolled in bed and kicked her grandmother.

"What's wrong with you tonight? If you're going to be like this to sleep with, you'll be on a pallet on the floor." Granny yanked the sheet straight.

"I'm sorry. I can't sleep. I've been thinking about Mother's letter. Granny, did you love Grandfather right away, or did you come to love him?"

Granny sat up. Her gray hair shined like silver in the moonlight. "I knew that man was the one for me the moment I laid eyes on him. He had the deepest laugh. It settled in and claimed my heart."

"What if I never feel that way about the man father has picked out for me?" She swung her legs off the bed and stood. "I don't know what to do."

"You don't have to marry anyone you don't love. That's not how this family works."

Emmie crossed the small room to the window and stared at the moon. "What about the commandment to honor thy parents?"

"Your father isn't going to demand you marry the farmer. If you wrote and said you wanted to stay in Trenton, he'd give you his blessing. He wants the best for you. That's what a good father does for his children."

"Not go to Kansas? I don't know. I would miss my family."

"Think about it. They've been gone several months, and I haven't seen many tears streaking down your cheeks. Now, get back in bed, and be still. The morning will be here soon enough."

As Emmie crawled under the sheet, the thought of Rooster crowing under her old bedroom window made her smile. Would Julia appreciate the wake-up call? She fell asleep thinking about Landon and his house.

Emmie woke up with a headache. She'd overslept. Rooster hadn't woken her. That's right. She wasn't in her own room. She rolled over on the empty bed. Granny wasn't in the room. She must have let Emmie sleep. At least she hoped she hadn't been told to get up and then rolled over.

She pushed back the sheet and jumped out of bed. In a flurry, she took care of her morning routine despite the fact nothing was normal. Her brush sat on Granny's dresser, not her own. *Father, I need to get this grumpiness out of me before I leave this room. Please help me.* A sense of peace settled over her. Last night, she'd been shown the house of her dreams with the man she'd fallen in love with, but he wasn't meant for her.

In the morning, light illuminated last night's foolishness over Landon's behavior. Crying to Granny wouldn't change things, but her advice was sound. Once Emmie arrived in Kansas, she could decide on her own to marry the widower or not. Now that Landon would be moving into a big house with Julia, she'd ask him if he'd take in Walter and Milton. They could learn to pick up their rooms and eat in the café. Surely Landon would understand her need to leave, and she wanted herself and Granny on that train by next week.

She tried hard to ignore the rock-crushing ache in her heart as she stepped into the kitchen.

There was her grandmother snuggled in Walter's arms.

"Granny!"

Walter stepped back from her grandmother as if Emmie had struck him with a burning log.

"Now, Emmie. Settle down. I've something to say to you." Granny took her by the hand and navigated her to the kitchen chair. "You see, Walter and I are in love. I'm not leaving Trenton. He's asked me to marry him, and I said yes. You're welcome to stay here with us or catch a train to Kansas. It's up to you."

Emmie sprang to her feet. Tears stung her cheeks as she ran from the kitchen, the screen door banging behind her. It wasn't fair. After all she'd done to marry Walter off, he'd fallen in love with Granny right under Emmie's nose.

CHAPTER 18

EMMIE MADE IT TO the church steps. In her haste, she'd left her hat behind. She'd lost a few hairpins on her flight, and strands tickled her chin. She perched on the stone steps to think. Nothing had really changed, other than she was now free to leave. Emmie's father wouldn't worry about Granny living in the town she loved once she was married.

That meant Emmie could leave tomorrow if she wanted.

But she didn't want to. Now that the barriers to leaving had been removed, she didn't want to go. Even if she never found someone to love her, this was her town. She stood and smoothed her skirt. She'd wander to the side of the church and think about what to write to her parents. It would be cool under the tree, and she wouldn't be in plain sight.

Her mother would be heartbroken, or at least Emmie thought she would be. She didn't want to cause her mother pain, but how could she leave? Granny might not need

Emmie any longer, but she still had a home. Maybe Landon would hire her to work for him all the time, if she could stand being around him after he married Julia.

"Emmie?"

She turned. Landon stood at the edge of the yard. Almost as if by thinking of him, he'd appeared. Did he have to be so attractive? So perfectly kept?

He strolled toward her. "I missed you at breakfast."

"How did you find me?"

"Your grandmother knows you well. I'd like to know you even better." He stopped inches from her.

"But Julia wouldn't care for that."

"She doesn't matter. You do. Last night, you ran off before I could ask you an important question." He stepped closer.

"About the store?"

"No. Emmie." He reached for her hands.

She let him take them, enjoying the way they swallowed hers.

"Emmie Mueller. I'd like to kiss you, but first, I want to know if you'll marry me?"

Emmie swayed, then caught her balance. "Yes, please."

Landon pulled her close and kissed her. White sparks flashed behind her closed eyes. She'd heard her friends say they'd seen fireworks when kissed, but she hadn't believed it until now.

After the kiss, she couldn't catch her breath. "That was lovely."

"Yes, it was. I've wanted to do that since the first day I met you."

"Landon, I don't want to move to Kansas. I want to live in that big house and have a family of our own."

"Then we shall."

CHAPTER 19

Rooster crowed under Emmie's window. She'd miss him. After today, she'd wake up in the house Landon bought for them. The weeks had flown by as she decorated the inside of the house with lovely things from the store and waited for her mother and father to arrive for the wedding. And now the day was here. She shivered. In a few short hours, she'd be Mrs. Knipp.

Thunder blasted the sky apart. How could it rain on her wedding day? She moaned. She wanted it to be perfect, and now it would be a muddy mess.

Her bedroom door creaked as Granny peered inside. "Just because it's your wedding day doesn't mean you get to sleep in. Come on, child. Slip on your wrapper and have breakfast with your parents and me. I've sent Walter and Milton on an errand. They'll be back in time for the wedding, but for today, the boardinghouse is for the bride's family only."

"But, Granny, you and Walter are married. He's family now."

"Pshaw. He'll be fine. He's got his shadow with him. Come now, get a bite to eat, and we'll get you into that beautiful dress."

"But the rain! My dress will be a sodden mess during the reception."

"Let's not borrow trouble. It will work out, you'll see. God can dry up the ground if He wants."

Landon's chest swelled with joy as his stunning bride, holding on to her father's arm, walked down the aisle toward him. He'd made the right choice coming to this town. God knew long before he moved here that he'd find the wife he longed for in Trenton.

The rain drummed harder on the tin roof.

Emmie looked up and met his eyes.

He smiled, and she grinned back. Their reception wouldn't be the one she'd dreamed about in the church's side yard. But he knew his bride. He could almost see how happy she would be when they arrived at the store, and she saw how they had transformed it. This time, she wouldn't be in charge of setting up the dinner. Instead, he, Cyrus, Milton, and Walter had decorated, even pulling out imported linen tablecloths to cover the cases for the many bowls and platters of food. They'd moved shelves, put trinkets away, and hung streamers, all to transform his store into a place of celebration.

Nothing was too special for his homegrown bride.

Don't miss another one of Diana's books sign up for her newsletter. Give me the News!

Not quite ready to leave this small town?

Then pick up The Honey Bride. **Afraid of her own shadow and now she's in charge.**

Read it now! Or if you're not sure here's a peek.

CHAPTER 20

The Honey Bride Chapter One

Wind-whipped water plopped on, splattered, and then moistened Katie Tucker's forehead, rousing her. Something wasn't right. She'd fallen asleep with open windows, hoping for a breeze to relieve the early summer heat. Now the wind was wicked, pulsating against the bedroom panes and blowing in rain. She sat, reached for the window, and closed it with a bang.

The sky lit up once, twice. The hair on her arms stretched for heaven. *Crack*. The second story sizzled and popped. Lightning. She shivered. Was it a tornado, like the one she'd read about last month? Five people in Wabash County had died.

Papa would be yelling to get to the cellar any minute. *Please, God, not down there*. Chill bumps raced up her arms.

Henry, her younger brother, banged against her door and called out, jarring her from the nightmare of spider webs stuck in her hair.

Had he said fire? In the house? The barn? Shaking, she fumbled for her wrapper, found it, then rushed her arms through the sleeves. Her shoes were by the back door. Henry waited at the bottom of the stairs.

"The barn's on fire. Papa's out there."

"Get a bucket! I'll get the stew pan. Where's Oma?"

"Sleeping."

"I'll wake her. Get as many things filled with water as you can." Henry's boots pounded sharply against the wood floor in time to her heartbeat. She needed to wake her grandmother.

Oma met her at the doorway.

"What's the yelling about?"

"Lightning started a fire in the barn. Papa is getting out the animals. I was coming to wake you."

"I'm up. Go help. I'll be there as soon as possible."

Katie hesitated. Should she insist her grandmother stay inside?

"Go, *Schatzi*. Now."

Her grandmother's strong words urged her feet forward, and she hightailed it down the stairs. She trembled on the bench, trying to get her shaking fingers to work her laces into place. The unnatural noises from the animals made her want to run back to bed. No matter how fearful she was, she couldn't. There was work to be done.

Outside, the smoke lay heavy in the air. They needed help. The farmhand Papa hired hadn't shown up. If they could get word to the fire department, but they were too far from town. She'd send Henry to the Gibbons'. They were the closest.

Henry worked the pump, water pouring, splashing against the bucket sides.

"Where's Papa?"

"Still in there. He got Starlight out first."

"Good. Get on her, ride to the Gibbons, and tell them we need help."

"I can help."

"We need more than the three of us. Hurry. You're faster than me."

Henry ran for the horse. Katie picked up the bucket of water Henry had filled. The handle bit into her hands as she carried it to the barn. "Papa! I have water!"

"I'm here." He grabbed the bucket and ran inside. Seconds later, he was back. "Fill it again. Hurry." He coughed. "Where's Henry?"

"I sent him for help." Flames licked the inside of the dry barn wood.

"They won't make it before it's burned to the ground." Her father bent over, coughing. When he was able to catch his breath, he handed her his kerchief. "Wet that and bring it with the next bucket. Lady Jane is still in there."

She shuddered. Lady Jane was difficult on a good day. In a fire, who knew what the horse was capable of doing.

Unable to sleep, Pete Dent paced the Gibbons' barn, where he slept. The rhythm of the rain didn't bring its usual soothing. Storms didn't bother him, but this one did. Too soon, too dangerous, after the one last month. He stood at the open door and noticed Roy standing on the porch. He jogged across the yard and up the steps. "Thunder keeping you awake?"

"Scared Frances. Alma's taking care of her." Roy said.

Crack. The lightning startled both men.

"That was close. Sounded like it hit something." Roy ran to the edge of the porch.

Pete looked the other way, toward the Tucker place. Katie on his mind again. He'd like to get to know her better. It had taken him a few months, but he'd managed to get her to smile at him at church, anyway. Shy little thing. He'd been ready to pull up stakes and find another place to work when she'd caught his eye. Katie might be the one person to tip the scale and keep him in Trenton.

"Do you see that?" Roy pointed in the direction Pete had been staring.

"That's a bright light. Too bright. Think they got hit with that last bolt?" Pete's heart pounded. "I'm riding out. They might need help if it hit the house or barn."

"Go. I'll let Alma know and meet you."

Pete wasted no time saddling Biscuit and urging him to a gallop. As he grew closer to the Tucker's, he knew something was burning. Probably the barn with the way the flames were flicking the sky. Someone rode toward him. Katie coming for help? He slowed his horse.

"Hey, our barn's on fire. Can you help?"

"Henry, is that you?"

"Yeah, Pete. Katie told me to get you. Hurry! Papa's getting the animals out and. . ." Henry stopped to catch his breath.

"I heard you. That's where I'm headed. Roy's behind me."

Henry turned Starlight around.

Both horses stretched into a neck-to-neck race for the Tucker barn.

When they arrived, the smoke was thick, but the bright flames licked through, illuminating the night, revealing Katie lugging a bucket. Pete dismounted and tied Biscuit to the porch railing. He ran to Katie and pried her fingers from the handle. "Fill another one and keep filling. I'll get them to the barn. Roy's on his way."

"Papa's in there! I can't get to him."

Cold sweat trickled down his back. If Mr. Tucker was still in that barn, the odds were he wasn't coming out. *Please, God, let her father be alive.* He ran inside, keeping low. "Mr. Tucker! Holler your position!" The roaring flames sucked his words into silence. He tossed the water on a bale of hay and ran out, gasping for air.

Katie waited with a pan of water. He took it and rushed back inside. He had to find her father.

Katie sat on the back steps, hugging Henry close to her. Waiting. Most of their church congregation either stood in the yard or were in the house. Katie and Henry sat alone. She couldn't talk to anyone, not even Alma.

Pete Dent had been kind, explaining how her father probably inhaled too much smoke and couldn't breathe. He'd seen it before, serving with the volunteer fire department. He told her to take Henry inside, but she couldn't. If she left these steps, it would be real. So she clung to Henry and waited.

Tears rolled down her cheeks, bringing some relief to the sting from the smoke.

Find out what happens next in The Honey Bride!

Chapter 21

About the Author

Diana Lesire Brandmeyer writes historical and contemporary romances. She is the best-selling author of *Mind of Her Own*, *Frontier Legacy Brides series,* and *The Silverton Lake Romance series.* Once widowed and now remarried, she writes with humor and experience on the difficulty of joining two families, be it fictional or real life.

Please visit her webpage, www.dianabrandmeyer.com and sign up for her newsletter.

Historical

Small Town Brides Collection

Love Finds an Outlaw

The Christmas Wish

The Matchmaker Bride

The Honey Bride

From a Distance

Frontier Legacy Brides Collection

A Bride's Dilemma in Friendship, Tennessee

A Bride's Journey to the Colorado Territory

A Bride's Choice in Central City
Contemporary
Silverton Series

All in Good Time

A Time to Dance

A Time to Bake

A Time to Heal

A Time to Love Collection
Stand-Alone Books

Mind of Her Own

Hearts on the Road

www.ingramcontent.com/pod-product-compliance
Lightning Source LLC
Chambersburg PA
CBHW021232130726
47988CB00002B/934